Nadja Maril

Me, Molly Midnight
the artist's cat

With paintings and drawings
by Herman Maril

1977

STEMMER HOUSE
PUBLISHERS, INC.

Owings Mills, Maryland

Inquiries should be directed to
Stemmer House Publishers, Inc.
2627 Caves Road
Owings Mills, Maryland 21117

A Barbara Holdridge book
Printed and bound in the United States of America
First Edition

Published simultaneously in Canada
by George J. McLeod, Limited, Toronto

Library of Congress Cataloging in Publication Data

Maril, Nadja.
    Me, Molly Midnight, the artist's cat.

    "A Barbara Holdridge book."
    SUMMARY: A small cat named Molly Midnight re-
calls how she became painter Herman Maril's favorite
model.
    [1. Cats—Fiction] I. Maril, Herman. II. Ti-
tle.
PZ7.M3385Me   [E]   77-22708
ISBN 0-916144-15-1
ISBN 0-916144-16-X pbk.

50534

Me, Molly Midnight
the artist's cat

Suzanne and Cat

To my parents

Molly Midnight is the daughter of a Greenwich Village, New York, black cat and a Provincetown sealpoint tomcat. Although in the past we had a falling out, we have since made our peace. The following story was written with the help of Molly one windy Provincetown night. It is a true story, and I hope you enjoy reading it as much as I have enjoyed writing it.

Suzanne Nadja Maril

Me, Molly Midnight
the artist's cat

I was not born with paint on my paws. But you might think so, seeing me now and knowing where I was born.

I spent my first days in Provincetown. That is a small town on Cape Cod where many painters live and visit. But as a newborn kitten, I never dreamed that someday the life of an artist's model would be for me—me, Molly Midnight!

Provincetown is built right beside the sea. At night I could hear the sound of the waves lapping against the shore. In the salt sea air was the good smell of fish. I loved Provincetown.

Artists love Provincetown, too. They come to Provincetown to see the special light reflected off the water. The light makes bright shades of blue and green, orange and tan. Back in their studios, the artists catch the brilliance of that special light in their paintings.

As a kitten I never noticed the special light. I was too busy playing with my four brothers and sisters. Our favorite game was hide-and-seek. We used to play it in the kitchen. We lived in an apartment with our mother, who was a black cat like me. I always found the best hiding places. My favorite was underneath the refrigerator. I always used to run there when I was scared.

I was under the refrigerator the day a little girl named Suzanne came with her mother. They wanted to pick out a kitten to take home with them.

"I want a black kitty," Suzanne told her mother. "Black all over, with no white hairs, and she has to be a girl."

I was the only black female in the litter. Even though I was hiding under the refrigerator, Suzanne found me.

"This is the kitten I want," said Suzanne to her mother. "See, she's all black."

I wailed when the girl put me inside a basket to carry me off to some strange place I didn't know. I didn't want to leave my mother and my brothers and sisters.

Off Shore

"What do you have in the basket?" Suzanne's father asked when they got me to their home.

"My little black kitten." The little girl took me out of the basket. "I'm going to call her Molly Midnight because she's black as midnight."

"She's kind of cute, there, with those big ears," her father said, laughing. "But I'm a dog man. I don't care too much for cats."

"Well, I do," retorted Suzanne, and she carried me upstairs to show me her room.

Suzanne and I spent a lot of time together. She liked to carry me around on her shoulder. That was fun, especially because I could see the tops of chairs and tables for the very first time. What great landing places they would make when I was grown enough to jump up on them!

Sometimes we played chase-the-paper-on-the-string. It was a game Suzanne made up all by herself. First she would tie a piece of paper to a string. Then she would run all around the room letting it trail behind her. I would run and jump in the air chasing it.

At night we slept in the same bed. Often I would climb up on Suzanne's shoulder and suck her ear. It reminded me of my mother's teat and helped me to fall asleep. Soon, I was almost as happy as when I lived with my mother and my brothers and sisters.

At the end of the summer, Suzanne and her family took me with them to their home in the city. Suzanne went back to school, and now I was left home alone. I had no one to play with, no one to carry me around. I felt so sorry for myself that I wanted to curl up in a corner and hide my face under my paws, but that really didn't seem an interesting way to spend

The Blue Pitcher

the day. I decided, instead, to explore the whole house.

I followed Herman, Suzanne's father, down a flight of stairs. There I discovered a large room with strange odors. I know now that they were the smells of turpentine and paint. Large cloths stretched on wood strips—called canvases—lined the walls. Some of the canvases were bare and white. Others were painted with colors and black lines.

Herman took a brush, dipped it into a color, and started painting something onto a canvas. The canvas he was painting was on a stand made of wood. I learned its name when I got tangled up with its three legs. "Watch my easel!" Herman shouted. I ran and hid under a pile of boxes. When I finally peeked out, I saw Herman lower the canvas on the easel. Then he raised it. He even tilted it at different angles. Finally he began to paint again.

As if by magic, the black painted lines became outlines of something. After a while Herman filled them in with color, and the brush strokes became a picture. Herman was an artist. I came out from my hiding place and purred to show my delight. But Herman paid no attention to me.

Usually, while Herman was painting in his studio, Suzanne's mother, Esta, was in her office talking to people. I once heard her say to a friend of Suzanne's that she was a social worker and helped people with their problems.

Esta fed me milk and fish and all kinds of good food. When I was full I liked sitting on the window sills. I could chew on the plants there, and I could bask in the sunlight. The sun's warmth felt good. I felt so cold and lonely with no one to play with!

I did enjoy prowling around the house, looking into all the corners and finding new things to do. Sometimes I tried to get attention by scratching the furniture. But most of the time I liked to curl up on a bright orange cushion and sleep.

One day while Herman and Esta were talking in the living room, they noticed me stretched out on a big curved chair.

"What a beautiful sleek cat Molly has grown into," Esta said to Herman.

But all Herman could say was, "Well, at least her ears don't look so big now that she's gotten larger."

"Herman, you should put Molly in a painting! Look how beautiful she looks in that red chair—her black fur stands out so against the red. And the curve of her body is almost like the curve of the chair."

"I'll decide what I want to paint. Leave me alone," he grumbled. But he did look at me in a new way, with his eyes narrowed as though he were con-

Duet

centrating. "Kind of interesting composition," he muttered to himself. "But there are better things to paint than cats."

Downstairs on his easel was a picture of himself. It was really two pictures of him in one painting: his face in a mirror and also in a self-portrait on an easel. Such a painting was something new for Herman. Most of his paintings were pictures of the sea and the sand dunes and the shorelines of Provincetown; he seemed to like wide open spaces. But if he could paint a picture of himself, I thought, he could paint a picture of *me*. I decided to make him notice me, and I planned how I was going to do it.

Herman began whistling, but he stopped short when I came over to him and asked, in my way, to be petted.

"Meow," I cried.

I began to rub myself against his leg and to purr. I liked the smell of paint on his trousers, so I jumped onto his lap. Next, I perched my front paws on his shoulders. I wanted to smell his mustache. It smelled like the kippers he'd had that morning for breakfast. I do so love fish. I began to purr more loudly. I liked the way he smelled and I liked his mustache. Suddenly I knew I was in love. My plan just had to succeed!

"It looks like Molly really likes you," Esta said to Herman.

"Likes me, she loves me!"

I sat on his lap, purring contentedly. Herman smiled and stroked my back. Finally I had found someone else in the family to be my friend, someone who would play with me.

A few days later when Herman was taking the cellophane off a piece of candy, I perked up my ears at the sound of the rustling paper. He rolled the cellophane into a ball and threw it for me to chase, and I ran to fetch it and bring it back to him. I chased the ball and brought it back again and again.

"Look, Esta!" Herman called. "I've taught Molly to chase the ball of cellophane and bring it back to me. She can retrieve. Come on, Molly. Show Mother how you bring me the cellophane," he coaxed.

Once again I performed.

I liked being Herman's cat. This made me special. I got to retrieve for him and explore his studio while he was painting. Someday, I thought, he will paint *my* picture. I liked hiding behind the paintings lined up against the wall and jumping on top of the different tables to sniff his paint and brushes.

Feline Domain

Looking In

I no longer considered myself Suzanne's cat. Now I preferred to spend the night snuggled between Herman and Esta, in their big bed. To make it clear whose cat I was, I refused to let Suzanne pet me. When she tried to pick me up I would even growl at her. Occasionally I would even chase her and claw mischievously at her legs.

Often Suzanne would bring her guitar into the living room to play and sing for her parents.

"I want you to hear a new song," she announced one evening.

Herman and Esta stopped their conversation to listen. I, however, looked with distaste at Suzanne singing and playing her guitar. I didn't want her to be the center of attention. So I sneaked over to where she was sitting and nipped at her knee.

"Ouch!" Suzanne cried. "That does it! Molly is no longer *my* cat. *You* can have her!"

Herman and Esta looked at each other and laughed.

"Then Molly will be *my* cat," Herman—*my* Herman—responded.

I pretended to be very busy washing my paws. But as soon as Suzanne left the room I jumped up onto Herman's lap to give him a kiss. I kissed him on the mustache. My plan had been a success.

Cat and Candelabra

Once I officially became Herman's cat, I spent even more time in his studio. I liked watching him work. He would concentrate hard on what he was painting. At the same time he looked happy, even serene. When Herman liked something he had completed, he would smile and nod his head.

I also liked spending my mornings with Herman, especially when he was eating breakfast. I always managed to get him to share with me when we were alone together. It became a game.

First I would nudge his leg and plaintively meow.

He would respond by saying, "What's the matter, Molly?"

"Meow," I would answer before jumping into his lap.

"Get off my lap," he'd tell me gruffly, pushing me off.

Then, with my fur a bit ruffled, I would start walking away, tail high in the air.

"All right, Molly," he'd say, "I'll share with you. Here's a kipper. Now behave yourself."

Once I got a few kippers down my throat, I would purr loudly to show my gratitude.

"Did you like those, Molly?" he would inquire.

Then I would purr even more loudly.

"Here, have another." And he would smile and take another sip of coffee.

"Well, Molly, I think after I finish this cup of coffee I'm going down to my studio to paint." That was his way of inviting me to come along.

Then it happened—just the way I had always hoped it would!

"Would you like to be my model?" Herman asked me one day.

"Meow," I said.

Being an artist's model means posing in one position for long stretches of time. I was already very good at staying in one position, because I could pose and sleep at the same time.

My favorite posing place was an old, warm radiator. I was always certain of being admired when I was lying there, because the white color of the radiator provided a good contrast with my black fur.

"Look at that cat," a guest at the house remarked one day. "She looks as though she's posing for a picture."

"Oh, Molly Midnight is just showing off," Suzanne retorted. "I think she looks like a fuzzy old caterpillar with five legs!"

"You're just jealous of Molly," her mother teased.

To cut short the argument, Herman interrupted. "Have you seen my new painting? It's got Molly in it. Come down to the studio."

Languid Cat

I followed them down the stairs. And suddenly everyone was making a bigger fuss about me than ever before.

"It's beautiful!" Esta commented as she gazed at the painting of me, Molly Midnight, sitting by an open door.

I turned and studied the picture. Herman had already painted me—and I had never even known it! A nice likeness, I observed, but the tail in the picture was too short. I'd have to do something about that.

Later, when everyone else had left the studio, I brushed against the painting with my own tail. The paint was still wet, and brushing the paint with my tail made the tail in the painting longer and furrier-looking. Now that's better, I thought, surveying my work. There's nothing sillier than a cat with a tail that's too short! But would Herman notice?

Early next morning, I ran down to see. He was studying the painting. I looked at him. He looked at me.

"You wouldn't know who's been messing around with my painting, would you, Molly?" he asked sternly.

"Meow," I answered. I would never tell! Not me, Molly!

Helping out with Herman's painting made me want to do a whole painting myself. Now that I was an artist's model, why couldn't I be an artist?

That afternoon while Herman was eating lunch, I jumped up on his palette, where he squeezed out his paints of various colors to mix them. I wetted my paws. I put a different color on each paw. I liked the blues and greens because they reminded me of the sea. Then I stepped onto a sheet of paper lying on the floor. But when I put the paint on paper, as I had seen Herman do, I found that the only pictures I could make were of paw prints. And worse than that, I

couldn't get the paint off me. I ran all over the house, getting my paw prints on everything. Finally Herman saw me and cleaned my paws with turpentine.

"Molly Midnight, what a dumb thing to do!" was all he said. "I'm the painter, not you."

Since I myself couldn't paint, I had to content myself with being painted.

When I looked at one of the pictures of me in the studio, I felt the same kind of peace and contentment I saw on Herman's face when he had finished a painting. It made me happy. And I soon found out that it could make other people feel happy, too.

The Palette

I discovered this one day when a curator from a large museum came to look at Herman's pictures. She was the person in charge of choosing paintings for the museum. That morning the house seemed very busy, with Esta preparing lunch for the visitor and Herman getting his studio in order.

As soon as I heard Herman welcome the guest at the front door, I came dashing down the stairs chasing a ball of yarn.

"That's quite a cat you've got there," the curator said. "What's her name?"

"Oh, that's Molly Midnight, my star model."

"I can see why. She's got a beautiful coat of fur. I hope I can see a painting of her."

"Would you like to come down to my studio?" Herman's eyes twinkled in that way I love.

"I'd like that. You lead the way," said the curator.

I had begun to settle down for a nap, but once the two had left, I decided to follow them. I was curious to learn what they were up to.

"I admire the way you use color in your compositions," the curator was saying as she looked at the paintings. "The colors make the subjects seem to float in space."

The paintings were some of those he had done in Provincetown. I remembered the good smell of the fish and the sounds of the sea. The special light in the paintings brought all those memories back to me.

Sand Bars

Interior with Cat

Then I saw the curator smile. I realized that she was sharing that special feeling of happiness which had come over me—that the paintings were somehow making her feel part of the place I had known. But how would she feel about the painting of me in the open doorway, the painting of me, Molly Midnight—the one *I* had painted?

Herman brought out my painting.

"*That's* the painting I want to hang in the museum," she said firmly as soon as she saw it. "What a feeling of serenity it has, with the little black cat in the midst of all that space!"

"Well, here's my model now."

I walked softly into the room and sniffed the air. I stretched myself out on the carpet so that they could see all the lines of my body.

"Molly posed especially for this painting."

The curator nodded. But I could tell that she wasn't really listening to what Herman was saying. She was too busy thinking about how beautiful *Interior with Cat* would look hanging in her museum.

Herman took a big breath. "In fact," he went on, looking directly at the cat's tail in the painting, "she really made quite a *special* contribution."

I came and sat by Herman's feet.

"You know what I mean, don't you, Molly?" he asked.

I purred, Herman winked, and we exchanged secret smiles.

Paintings by Herman Maril in this book

The Blue Pitcher, oil painting, 1975, collection of Herman Maril, Baltimore, Maryland

Cat and Candelabra, oil painting, 1971, collection of Esta Maril, Baltimore, Maryland

Duet, oil painting, 1973, collection of Jules Horelick, Baltimore, Maryland.

Feline Domain, oil painting, 1975, collection of Herman Maril, Baltimore, Maryland

Interior with Cat, oil painting, 1972, courtesy of the National Collection of Fine Arts, Smithsonian Institution, Washington, D.C.

Languid Cat, oil painting, 1976, collection of Herman Maril, Baltimore, Maryland

Looking In, oil painting, 1976, collection of Herman Maril, Baltimore, Maryland

Off Shore, oil painting, 1966, courtesy of the Baltimore Museum of Art, Baltimore, Maryland

The Palette, oil painting, 1976, collection of Herman Maril, Baltimore, Maryland

Sand Bars, oil painting, 1963, courtesy of the Baltimore Museum of Art, Baltimore, Maryland

Suzanne and Cat, oil painting, 1962, collection of Irvin Greif, Jr., Pikesville, Maryland

The cat shown with Suzanne is her first cat, Silkie, a Truro silver tabby given to her by her Provincetown neighbor Phil Alexander.

Me, Molly Midnight,
   the Artist's Cat

Designed by H. L. Perlman Associates

Composed by the Service Composition Company, Baltimore, Maryland
   in Century Expanded with Torino Roman Swash display

Color separation by Graphic Technology, Fort Lauderdale, Florida

Printed by the John D. Lucas Printing Company, Baltimore, Maryland
   on 80 lb. Mead Special Opaque, Regular Finish

Bound in paper by the John D. Lucas Printing Company, Baltimore, Maryland

Hardbound in Kivar 5 Kerry Green, Linenweave, by Complete Books Company,
   Philadelphia, Pennsylvania